ANTIGONE

ANTIGONE

Hollie McNish

FLEET
2021

FLEET

First published in Great Britain in 2021 by Fleet

1 3 5 7 9 10 8 6 4 2

All rights whatsoever in this play are strictly reserved and application
for performance etc. should be made before rehearsals by professionals and by
amateurs to Lewinsohn Literary Agency, 58 Old Compton Street, London, W1D 4UF.
Mail to: becky@lewinsohnliterary.com. No performance may be
given unless a licence has been obtained.

A CIP catalogue record for this book
is available from the British Library.

ISBN 978-0-349-72718-9

Typeset in Garamond by M Rules
Printed and bound in Great Britain by Clays Ltd, Elcograf S.p.A.

Papers used by Fleet are from well-managed forests
and other responsible sources.

Fleet
An imprint of
Little, Brown Book Group
Carmelite House
50 Victoria Embankment
London EC4Y 0DZ

An Hachette UK Company
www.hachette.co.uk

www.littlebrown.co.uk

FOREWORD BY THE AUTHOR

*A single word frees people of all weight and
pain of life, and that word is love.*

– SOPHOCLES

I was approached to reimagine the play that you are about to read –
possibly in bed or a big bubble bath because you fancied something
ancient to delve into, or maybe you are being forced to read it
awkwardly in front of your class by a keen teacher – by a lovely
guy called Alex Clifton, then Artistic Director of Storyhouse,
Chester, UK.

Alex himself is a sunbeam of a human who, many times now
during my career, has encouraged me to work on projects that
initially I didn't feel too confident about. As well as Alex being
lovely, Storyhouse is one of my favourite theatres, largely because
it is a beautiful library (with a great children's section), cinema,
theatre and café in one – and for this reason one of the least
intimidating theatre spaces I've been in. Despite all this, when
Alex first asked me I said no thank you. I don't want to work
on *Antigone*.

I said no, first and foremost, because I did not feel qualified to reimagine *Antigone* – a play written over two thousand years ago by one of the most enduring playwrights of ancient Greece.

I have not studied theatre, I told Alex. I was not in any school play, save being a shepherd in the Primary nativity, tea-towel thrown on my head for extra credibility. Perhaps more importantly, I thought, I am not really a 'theatre-goer', as people say. I had seen, before working on this play, perhaps twenty plays in my entire life. During my childhood and into adulthood, most of the plays I saw were pantomimes or musicals, an outing maybe once a year with family or friends as a Christmas treat. And it was a treat. I loved them, and still do, especially *The Rocky Horror Picture Show, Joseph and the Amazing Technicolor Dreamcoat* and most recently the Tina Turner musical. *Antigone*, on first reading, did not seem to be this sort of play; not the sort of play I 'got'. It was, as I put it at the time, 'serious theatre' and I did not have a great track record with 'serious theatre'. (By this term, I mean theatre with more serious, less comedic themes, or at least serious themes spoken not sung – I am not implying pantomimes or musicals are not serious art. I firmly believe they are and should be credited as such.)

So, musicals and Christmas pantos aside, I have often found theatres fairly intimidating spaces, so much so that I've paid to get into my own poetry gig before for fear of telling the person at the front of house that I was actually the main performer.

Other scuffles with 'serious' theatre shows have also increased this feeling of trepidation. Not the plays themselves, so much as the whole experience within these spaces. Examples (in no particular chronological order) include having been glared at for taking a quiet sip from an apple juice carton; been scowled at by a fellow audience-member for opening a packet of crisps, and feeling so awkward about making any tiny noise that instead of chewing them I just sort of sucked each crisp quietly into tasteless mush and swallowed; having been looked up and down by a group of very well-dressed people (I assumed for being a bit scruffy but it may not have been this and I may just have imagined it because I felt awkward and under-dressed in the theatre a lot of the time); and, going back to early childhood, having been forced by my loving parents, when I was about eight, to wear a red velvet pinafore and floaty white blouse (that my gran had bought me and which I absolutely hated) because my school was taking us to see a play and I 'had to look my smartest for the theatre'. My mum recalls fondly that before this school trip I shut myself in our bathroom screaming 'I don't want to wear that horrible dress'. I wore it in the end but sat watching the play refusing to unbutton my anorak. From a young age, serious theatre seemed to involve wearing clothes you felt uncomfortable in in order to look like you were something you weren't and being quieter than was humanly possible. I longed for the popcorn freedom of the cinema.

In later years, I did start to appreciate the theatre trips my parents took me on, but I still wasn't great at the seriousness – neither were they. My most vivid memory in this respect was being told off as a teenager by a woman in the row in front of us at the *Swan Lake* ballet.

My mum had taken two of my school mates and me to see the ballet – a 'cultural experience' – but as soon as it started, a dancer leapt across the stage with tights so pale white and tight you could see the shadow of his penis. My mum and I immediately started giggling hysterically. Then both my friends started giggling until we were all stifling our immature sobs into our palms instead of concentrating on the extremely beautiful dancing. The woman in front of us eventually turned around (fair enough, we were literally unable to deal with watching one man in ballet tights and she had paid the same ticket price as us to watch the show), and hissed 'for goodness' sake, be quiet or leave', which of course made us even more giggly. We were in the wrong here, I do know that, but I also think that our laughter was made worse by our nervousness in trying to be so well-behaved initially.

What I guess I'm saying is that I have often felt I've had to be on my very best behaviour whilst watching serious plays, not only in the standard polite and respectful way that shared public spaces warrant, but in a more awkward, intimidated way too. It wasn't 'fun'. Often, despite the cushioned seats, it wasn't even comfortable. It was something I did because my parents told me it was good for me or because it was deemed a 'cultural experience' that would somehow make me a 'better' person or because I was studying the play at school and the class went on a trip. As I became an adult, my prejudice was hard to shift. Musicals and pantomimes brilliant, but anything more serious than that and I was probably not going to understand it, or at the least be told off for something.

The word 'cultural' also started to grate. Why was viewing certain art deemed 'a cultural experience'? A classical music concert, yes. A Shakespeare play, yes. An opera or a ballet, yes. Yet when I danced to Little Mix in concert, or watched the England versus Germany Women's World Cup match, or sat in awe as Kevin Bridges made a room full of five thousand people laugh hysterically simply by telling stories on a stage, not so much. I did a gig for Cambridge University once. It was at the Museum of Anthropology and Archaeology. I find this museum fascinating and for some reason spent loads of time there when I was pregnant. I was very excited about this gig. I read my poems for half an hour to a crowd of invited guests amongst an array of artefacts spanning two million years of history. After the gig, a man came up to me and congratulated me on the reading.

He then said: *It's so refreshing to hear such non-culture in such a cultural setting.* I'm still not sure how he expected me to take that as a compliment. Perhaps he didn't. I called up my mum laughing. Non-culture! What a bloody cheek!

A final confession to Alex to cement my refusal of the *Antigone* offer: with the exception of Simon Godwin's 2015 production of *Hamlet* at the RSC, starring Paapa Essiedu in the title role, Sabrina Mahfouz's *A History of Water in the Middle East* and an extraordinary 'immersive theatre experience' my boyfriend took me to see which was set in a pitch black shipping container, I had rarely been to watch a serious play that hadn't made me sleepy, by which I mean I often fell asleep in theatres, added proof I should stick to other art forms. Long play plus comfy seats plus warm theatre plus being forced to stay absolutely still and silent for two hours was a sure-fire way to knock me out. In fact, the first time I saw *Hamlet*, when I was fourteen, I fell asleep for about an hour. My parents had taken me but I'm not exactly sure why because it was a four-hour version and I wasn't even studying it at school (in my head this is the only reason I'd have ever gone to see a Shakespeare play as a teenager). I fell asleep after roughly an hour and when I woke up there was a naked man (Hamlet) dancing around the stage, his penis flailing in all directions. It was definitely my favourite part of the play, probably because I had been asleep for a lot of the rest of it and well, because he was naked and seeing a penis no-handed helicoptering like that was a rare treat.

In much more recent years, I have been to watch several incredible and life-changing plays, thanks mainly to my mother and my boyfriend encouraging me to 'branch out a bit' during the Edinburgh festival, where you can see more theatre in a week than you (or I) normally can in a year. But for me there is still a tingle of stigma that a lot of theatre is somewhat unwelcoming to the general public – and I desperately did not want to be part of this.

I cautiously told Alex all this.

He said, Great. Can you do it then?

I said, I'm not sure. On top of all my other inhibitions, I didn't know if I wanted to work on this play specifically.

I had read three different adaptations of *Antigone* twice each and watched three online productions and although I found many parts extremely captivating – especially Tiresias's speeches in Seamus Heaney's version and the dialogues between Ismene and Antigone in Anne Carson's version – I didn't love the play at first. I found it fairly miserable. I know, I know, it's a Greek tragedy. I wasn't expecting Mary Poppins on ice. But the world is miserable enough, I thought. And being a writer is already quite an isolating career. To be blunt, I didn't know if I wanted to sit at a desk on my own, surrounding myself with a play filled with grief and death, for months, maybe longer.

A very dear friend had also died to suicide shortly before I read *Antigone*, and I wasn't sure whether this play, in being so full of this form of death, perhaps made light of it somehow; even glamorised it for dramatic effect. I especially hated the references to hanging and was worried about the specific details given in some of the translations; the sort of detail we now ban from newspaper stories for fear of copycat culture. That said, Greek theatre was also extremely strict about depictions of violence or suicide, all of which were 'performed' offstage and reported on stage by messengers, in contrast to a lot of what we are used to seeing visualised in film and television today.

Still, I told Alex my concerns. He said: well, change those bits. This is a reimagining, Hollie.

If I'm honest, at this point I hadn't much of a clue what a 'reimagining' really meant.

So I can change it then? I said.

Yes! It's a reimagining, he repeated.

So I started to play around with it. The thought of messing with Sophocles felt ridiculous; arrogant even, but also fairly exciting. Over two thousand years this play has lasted and here I am, sat at a little desk by my bed with a pencil in my hand scoring out chunks of the writing like 'nah, take that bit out', or 'too repetitive, Sophocles' or 'no-one would understand this now', and so on. When I was working late at night, I sometimes imagined Sophocles pacing the room fuming at me, attempting to grab the pencil with his phantom fingers. Then I thought he'd probably have better places to be than my bedroom.

I read various translations over again. I researched more about Sophocles himself. I researched more about the story of *Antigone*, which I knew zero about initially. I finally started to enjoy the story, to appreciate the beauty of the language, once I wasn't spending my entire reading time googling 'who is Hades?', 'who is Oedipus's wife?', 'who is Danae?', 'what is the house of Labdacus?', 'where is Argos in relation to Athens?', 'how many affairs did Zeus have and how do Gods have sex anyway?' (This last one was less to do with the play and more personal intrigue.) I giggled at certain parts – the Messenger's breathlessness, the chattering or gossiping nature of the Chorus.

I found myself shouting at the TV as I watched Donald Trump's final speeches as US president, 'that's just like Kreon on page . . .!' And again, whilst watching re-runs of *The Office*, I wondered whether Sophocles would have recognised some of Kreon in David Brent's tragic ego, some of his insecurities too, perhaps. And what about Tiresias and *Game of Thrones*' Bran

Stark? I think they would have got on well. I found myself poring through speeches online and obsessing over the pairing up of words spoken by these ancient characters and the modern day politicians and activists I was brought up learning from. How closely some of Antigone's lines on law-abidance echoed Martin Luther King's most famous warnings. Or Vanessa Nakate's and Greta Thunberg's more recent laments on the need to shake politicians into action on the environment. I put on the radio and as Alicia Keys' 'Girl on Fire' sang loudly through my kitchen the lyrics shook me – 'that's Antigone!' I got very excited.

Instead of thinking: why aren't we focusing on new work rather than regurgitating old plays written two thousand years ago, I started to find it incredible, and also deeply depressing, that so many of the themes of *Antigone* are still so relevant today: the position of women in society; the unjust power of monarchy; the belittling treatment of the working classes; the use of many men in war as 'battle fodder'; the effect of power on the ego of those who are given it; the importance of speaking up against injustice and the difficulty so often in safely doing so. Two thousand years and so little seemed to have changed. I read the final lines of the play about wisdom and burst. I read the opening scene again and was comforted by the fact that the stage direction – two women alone outside – would no longer shock most modern audiences. So some things have definitely changed.

Saying this, this play stood out in ancient Greek times because it had a central female protagonist – not only that, but two *named* female characters who speak to each other about something other than a man. A large proportion of modern cinema still doesn't pass this basic Bechdel test. *Antigone* does. Two thousand years. Seriously.

As well as the story of the play itself, once I could read it without a dictionary beside me, the research which cemented my desire to give this 'reimagining' a go was into Greek tragedy and Greek theatre more generally. It calmed all my concerns about crisp-eating.

I read that *Antigone*, as with most of the tragedies in ancient Greece, was often put on as part of religious festivals, the most revered of which was the Great Dionysia. This was essentially a festival celebrating pleasure in honour of Dionysus, the Greek God of many things pleasure-related including fertility, phalluses, wine and ... theatre. Theatre! Tragic Theatre was seen as a godly pleasure alongside kissing and feasting and possessing a magic cup constantly refilling with wine. I wish I had known this when I was sucking the salt off more soggy crisps during Scene 3 of *Richard III*.

I learnt that Greek tragedies tended to be put on during these festivals as part of a theatrical competition each year. For over fifty years, Sophocles was the most celebrated playwright of these dramatic competitions. Apparently, he never came lower than second place. There were often comedians on before the plays. The theatres were more like stadiums and the audiences not only weren't scowled at for eating a few crisps or giggling at a penis outline on some ballet tights, they were often actively encouraged to heckle, drink and feast, and their viewing experience sometimes began with a parade of several giant phalluses across the stage. I imagined Sophocles each year back to defend his Tragedy Title like a champion boxer cheered into the ring again.

Ancient Greek theatre began to fascinate me. I was jealous that Greek audiences got to sit and glug wine and woop and see comedians before watching these serious plays, whilst I was forced into uncomfortably smart dresses and silence to watch mine. Put into the context of these festivals, the tragedies came to life a little more. I imagined the excitement of the competition, the effect on audiences of the rather over the top nature of these tragedies. I started to see them (apologies Sophocles) as more akin to modern-day soap operas. Think *EastEnders* in togas before we had any sort of television at all. Or perhaps more as if soap operas were only shown once a year in a festival during which hundreds of us gathered around a giant screen to watch three different versions of the most dramatic Christmas episode of *EastEnders* one after the other with comedians doing a set in between whilst we sang drunkenly along to the theme tune and feasted ourselves on wine and chocolate in praise of Pleasure. I began to like the idea of Greek theatre a lot.

I don't think theatres can ever be like this again, because of course we now have so many forms of entertainment that didn't exist in ancient Greece. I also don't really want theatres to resort to the Dionysus days. Firstly, it is contested whether any women were allowed in to watch the plays, so I'd possibly not have seen any plays at all. Secondly, as well as the food and drink and festivities, it has also been suggested that these festivals encouraged human trafficking of people forced into sexual slavery to please a drunken male theatre audience – much like what occurs worldwide during World Cup football matches nowadays. Thirdly, I'm not really keen on us going back to pigs being sacrificed on stage or lines of young boys carrying a giant model penis to praise the God of fertility before each play (unless there's a giant clitoris alongside it perhaps). So not *everything* about Greek theatre appealed, but there was a lot that enticed me. It seemed to me (and I am in no way an expert here) a combination of tragedy, stand-up comedy, musical theatre, soap opera, football crowds and piss-up.

With all that in mind, I said yes, I'd love to work on this play and it is an absolute honour to be asked.

So for this reimagining, I have three main fixations.

Firstly, to keep *Antigone* as *Antigone*. By this, I mean that I did not want to shift this play into a different time or space; I did not want to replant the characters into other bodies. I wanted to tell Sophocles' story, this ancient Greek story, in the way I think Sophocles intended. Greek theatres were not full of props or costumes or fancy sets. They were made of stories and words and people. I love stories and words and people. This is a beautifully written ancient story that has outlasted thousands of orbits of the sun and we still have access to it. That's an incredible thing. I wanted to tell this story as best I could and do justice to the poetry that, so far as I can tell from the translations I have read, it was written in. Sometimes I imagine that all the words we speak, invisible as they are, stay suspended in the air, floating forever. How magical to think that some of the words written by Sophocles all those years ago might still be mingling together in the air, from the first actors that spoke these parts to those in theatrical reimaginings across the world today. Perhaps the audience heckling too.

Secondly, I wanted to give the play at least a hint of its competitive festival setting. This play would not have been watched in isolation by many of its original audiences, yet here we are now, plonking it on its own into a theatre for a couple of hours. What a very different experience it must have been to watch this in its competitive Dionysia glory days!

Finally, I desperately wanted this version of *Antigone* to be understood and enjoyed by a modern audience the way that an ancient Greek audience would most likely have been able to; I didn't want the audience sitting confused in their seats because they're not classical scholars or attendees of schools where ancient Greek culture is studied. I wanted anyone to be able to watch this play and get into it. I asked myself over and over again: What, as a modern audience member with zero knowledge of ancient Greek culture, stopped me from relating to this play initially? What made it more difficult for me to follow the story? And where's the line between elucidating the play for modern audiences who don't already know the background to *Antigone*, and simplifying the play or patronising an audience who do know a bit more? I'm still not sure of the answers to these questions, but I hope I have made a fair effort to get the balance right.

Here are some examples of the larger changes I made for this reason. I hope that Sophocles will forgive me.

1. As mentioned before, I removed the specific references to hanging. I also, after much deliberating, removed an entire character: Euridice. In the original play, Euridice is the mother of Haemon and wife of Kreon, King of Thebes. Her main action within the play is an extremely swift decision to end her own life. I won't tell you why because it will be a spoiler if you don't know the story. I deliberated for weeks over this decision. I discussed it a lot with Alex. Not only was I removing an entire character from this play, but, as a mother myself, and somebody who bangs on a lot about the need for more representation of motherhood in the arts, I was cutting the only mother out entirely. But I did, because I was worried about this portrayal of suicide the most. Perhaps this is ridiculous in a play filled with violence and incest, but a gut feeling is a gut feeling. Also, to be frank, I did not want the play to be quite so long and this was one of the sections I thought made the least difference when cut.

2. The play in my version opens with much more vulgar language from the character of Antigone than in the original. An

ancient Greek audience would likely have been shocked by the opening vision of a woman being outside alone. Most modern audiences would be utterly unaffected by this. Therefore, I wanted Antigone to use language in a way that would shock a modern audience when she first appears. The vulgar language is my attempt at a modern translation of the ancient Greek stage direction 'woman outside alone'.

3. I found a lot of the long monologues by the Chorus especially challenging. This was largely due to the fact that these sections of the play reference a huge number of Greek stories that I knew nothing about. Yes, whilst reading the play, I could look up who Danae or Lycurgus or Cleopatra or Hades were but if I were sat in the theatre I could not. I don't think it was Sophocles' intention to baffle audiences with these references. I had read that his audiences would have been largely clued up on these. When I mentioned this to a friend, she exclaimed 'you don't know who Hades is?' This didn't help. We can't all know everything. Some things I just don't know, even things which are, apparently, common knowledge. I'm sure, even if many modern audiences do know who Hades is, that there will undoubtedly be other references that they are not familiar with; references which would leave them confused and perhaps drifting in the theatre. So I have made quite drastic changes to both who the chorus represent and also to the stories they reference, in the hope of allowing an audience member like myself to continue to be immersed in the story. I also made the Chorus representative of the younger generations, in the hope of bringing out the theme of generational conflict and support. Finally, I wanted to add slightly more playfulness and humour to the Chorus. I think Greek

audiences would have derived this from the setting in which they watched the play or the comedians they possibly watched in between the plays. I wanted to let a modern audience laugh a little too.

4. With Alex's support, I have tried to accentuate the theme of 'environment / earth' in this version of *Antigone*. There are a lot of references to Gods in this play and there was a lot of discussion about what these references would invoke for a modern-day audience. The idea of the Gods' power is quite confusing in this respect because the Greek Gods are so different to much modern religious thought. So, I have given *Antigone* more language connected to nature in order to pull us away from these Gods as religious figures and emphasise their more natural earthly connections: Gods as Thunder / Sea / Death / Harvest / Pleasure etc. In the play, it is suggested that this God, our Earth (Gaia) is 'the main God'. Perhaps worshipping the Goddess Gaia for Greek audiences would be less linked to a modern-day religious experience and more closely related to environmentalist thought. At least, this is the direction I went in.

I have not tried to simplify *Antigone*. I have not tried to, and hope I have not inadvertently managed to 'dumb it down' in any way. I have simply tried to reimagine it in a way that puts modern audiences in a similar position to Sophocles' audiences – in terms of their understanding of the language, the themes and the references within it, as well as the spirit in which they'd likely be watching it.

I should warn you finally that the most famous speculation surrounding Sophocles' death at the age of ninety or ninety-one is that he died from the strain of trying to recite one of the longer sentences from *Antigone* without pausing to take a breath. I don't know which sentence it was exactly, so be careful when reading.

CHARACTER NOTES

Antigone: *daughter of Oedipus*
(age 9–25) In my head, Antigone hints at Vanessa Nakate, Malala, an older Greta Thunberg. She is very opinionated, believes deeply in her Gods (which are also here The Earth / The Environment) but can be found annoying to listen to all the time by some people. I don't want her totally likeable but I want us to sympathise with her. She puts on a strong front but is petrified and lonely. She often speaks in nature-driven metaphors.

Kreon: *new King of Thebes, uncle of Antigone and Ismene*
(age 40–60) If Kreon is the establishment – both monarch and state – personally it only works that he is male and middle-aged. If he is to be someone whose stubbornness softens too late, I think he has to represent, in appearance, the people we most often see making these sorts of decisions. Kreon's character curves throughout the play. At first, he is unsure, timid even, and for me, it is his being King which heightens his sense of authority and the certainty of his own decisions, which are then lost by the end. He often speaks in man-made metaphors – ships / bricks / walls – in contrast to Antigone. I want it obvious that it is the role of King which bolsters

his confidence and arrogance, which then causes his downfall, rather than an inherent character trait.

Ismene: *Antigone's sister*
Must be good at crying!

Haemon: *Antigone's fiancé, Kreon's son*
(age 19–25) The same age as Antigone. Not older. Haemon is an equal to Antigone in many ways and I want their similarity in age to depict that.

Tiresias: *A seer*
Any age. Could be interesting played by a young actor (think Bran Stark style wisdom or the young princess in *NeverEnding Story*) or an elderly wise person (am thinking the witch in *Robin Hood, Prince of Thieves* here or the *Romeo and Juliet* priest in the Baz Luhrmann film adaptation). In the original, Tiresias is blind but in this version this is not mentioned and a casting can decide.

The Chorus: *representatives of the younger general public*
(ages 1–18) I have differentiated between seven chorus members in the text. The only stipulation is that Chorus 1 should be the youngest member, Chorus 5 the eldest. Or, Chorus 1 the shortest and Chorus 5 the tallest, if they are all the same age.

Comedian / Compere:
Male. Able to do a solo stand-up comedy set in the bar pre-show (this is at the theatre's discretion but I think would create a great atmosphere pre-show), plus the hosting at the beginning of the play. Preferably a local accent.

Audience members 1, 2, 3:
Able to throw tomatoes and shout loudly. Dressed as any modern-day theatre audience so it's a shock to those around them in the seats. Could be played by Chorus members.

Guard

Messenger

ANTIGONE

(As people enter the theatre, the song 'Girl on Fire' by Alicia Keys is played on loop as loud background music. Alternatively this could be sung live)

(The year is 467 BC.* COMPERE stands in a single spotlight to address the audience)

COMPERE: **

Good evening, men of Greece!***
Welcome to the final play of this year's festival of
Dionysus

(If the audience doesn't cheer, which they likely won't as they're in a modern-day theatre, COMPERE tries to encourage them, makes a joke about the cheering not being quite good enough, asks if they are hungover from yesterday's feast etc. Makes them try it again)

As always, let us begin by thanking the great God of
Theatre himself.
Cups up.

(lifts goblet of wine)
Dear Dionysus
Thank you for all that you give us
which we so gratefully take

(sips wine)
Thank you, first, for these grapes

(sips)
for their glorious scent

(sips)
for fertility, our most able Goddess

(moves hips mock sexily)
for her kleitoris*
for our giant phalluses**
all their holy mortal pleasures

and of course, thank you, Amen
for Theatre!

(applause, can be pre-recorded but must be very loud, football stadium style)

For those at last year's Great Dionysia, I am sure you
will remember if you were not too intoxicated by
then, that for the first time in thirteen long years,
our previous reigning champion, *the* master of tragic
theatre, Aeschylus himself, was beaten by our new face
on the scene.

---

* *Clitoris* is said to come from the ancient Greek word 'kleitoris'.
** At this point, the compere either points to his own penis or to a small boy standing holding a giant penis statue or to a statue of a penis on stage. This Greek festival often included a procession of 'penis-carriers'.

(loud booing and cheering – again, pre-recorded)

> **AUDIENCE MEMBER NUMBER 1:**
> It was a fucking fix!*

> **AUDIENCE MEMBER NUMBER 2:**
> Aeschylus was stitched up.

> **AUDIENCE MEMBER NUMBER 3:**
> *(to the other audience members)*
> Oh fuck off, Sophocles won, get over it

> **AUDIENCE MEMBER NUMBER 1:**
> Sophocles is a goat shit!** He wouldn't know good
> theatre if it smacked him in the bollocks

(AUDIENCE MEMBER 1 launches a tomato from a basket at the COMPERE; a GUARD goes into the audience and drags them out as they fight one another over the other audience members)

---

* I want to start the play with a bit of heckling and general audience action. The original performance of this play would likely have been in an ampitheatre with huge and therefore very influential audiences. The Dionysian Theatre in Athens held up to fourteen thousand people. According to sources: 'Greek audiences were talkative and unruly. If they disliked a play, they would drum their heels on the benches, jeer loudly and throw fruit.' (Sarah Grochala, 'Ancient Greek Theatre', Headlong.co.uk, 2012, https://headlong.co.uk/ideas/ancient-greek-theatre/) Saying this, I find forced audience participation when I see a play very intimidating so to plant a few hecklers in the crowd was my idea of a compromise.

** *Gràson* was an ancient Greek insult meaning to stink like a goat.

3

EMCEE:
(ducking out of the way)
Calm yourselves, *gentle* /men.
It seems we need some housekeeping before we begin.

Everyone in the theatre is to be seated now
No more fighting in the back*
Keep your sacrificial pigs *on leads*
Hold your wine down if you can**
And if there are any . . .

(looks around the room slowly, scouring, disgusted look on face, spits, sees a few, remarks and points them out)

. . . women in this audience

(encourages them to stand up, points them out to everyone)
I'm told we've let you in to this one
Please be aware this will not set a precedent
for all future theatrical performances

Toilets are out the back, men
No pissing in the river

Now, as I was saying,
the final play of this year's festival of Dionysia

---

* maybe the compere points someone out here
** At this point, the compere could name a few people in the audience for comedic effect, if names of audience members are available (e.g. 'Especially you, Becky Thomas in Row 10' and so on.)

from last year's new champion of tragedy
is indeed:

drum roll please

Antigone by Sophocles

I've been told some background information may be
necessary for those of you who have come here all the
way from outside Greece. So welcome to our great
Athens once again and please pay attention.

*(pulls down a PowerPoint presentation or slide or equivalent. First
image is a map of Greece marked with Thebes and Athens. A large
arrow labelled 'You are Here' points to Athens)*

Our final play is *Antigone*. It is set in Thebes. Thebes is
a city in central Greece; a major rival of us Athenians.
The princess, Antigone, so the story goes, and her
family, are from Thebes. With me so far? Good.

(another slide comes down with ANTIGONE's family tree)

This is Antigone's family tree. It is a fairly complicated
history so listen closely.
Antigone's father is Oedipus, who you may have heard
of. He was the King of Thebes, until he found out that
his wife, Queen Jocasta, Antigone's mother, was also
his mother, which meant that for over a decade he had
been coming between the same thighs he came out
of, which was all very awkward. *(maybe sexual action*

5

here) So, what did Oedipus do? Poor man, he gouged both his eyes out with pins. Or his own fists. This detail is still in debate. It was the shame that killed him either way.

So Oedipus died, and his poor wife, Antigone's mother, who had also not realised till that moment that she had birthed four children with the man who was also her son, died soon after. You knew this was a tragedy so don't start complaining now.

(crosses appear over Oedipus's name and Queen Jocasta's)
So, Antigone's parents are dead, and their sons,
Antigone's only two brothers
(points to the family tree)
Eteocles and Polynices, become joint Kings of Thebes

(crowns appear over their names)
Unfortunately, these two brothers argue so much
about the leadership position
that they decide it best,
rather than form a Kingly coalition,
instead to take turns, year by year.
First up is Eteocles, the eldest,
Polynices next. Seems like a good plan?
(crown is taken from above Polynices' name)

Unfortunately, after one year, Eteocles
is still loving being King of Thebes
and does not want to hand over the crown
to his silly little brother
(crown flashes from name to name)
That is a problem.

Polynices gets annoyed, as you might imagine,
flees the city, gathers an enemy army from Argos,
and storms back to regain his rightful turn to wear the crown.

(sets aside the PowerPoint presentation; more animated
storytelling now)
Oh! The battle is a bloody and bitter one
with the Gods of Thunder *and* War both getting
involved;
soldiers from both sides extinguished like stars
until finally the people of this city,
sick of losing loved ones in yet another royal feud,
begin a public protest: 'This civil war must end
with a duel between the brothers!
This is their battle! Not ours!'

(slowing down then building drama)
And that, my men, is what happened.
Only hours before you arrived
armies on both sides gathered in silence
as these two brothers, Eteocles and Polynices,
took to the stage, stepped towards one another
swords pulled from their scabbards
and attacked each other

(pause)

Polynices died … first
Eteocles soon after
Both struck by
the other brother's blade

blood swapping blood
beneath the same scorched sun

(slower)
So here, we begin:
Both brothers have been killed
Their uncle Kreon is now king
The city is fresh from civil war
and Antigone
stands all alone outside the palace walls

(play begins)

ANTIGONE:

(screams into the audience, loud,
tired, almost given up) *

Exóloio! Exóloio! Bdelyros! **

(a little quieter now, to herself, but still screaming, breathless, repeating
until the word loses a little of its shock factor)

Fuck!

Fuck. Fuck.

(ISMENE walks quickly on stage, looking around nervously as she does
so, as if they should not be where they are, sees ANTIGONE)

ISMENE:

(whispering in an encouraging way for
ANTIGONE to whisper too)

Antigone?!

(no reply, whispers louder)
Antigone?!

---

* The tone I think of here is of Leonardo Di Caprio's line 'I defy you stars' in Baz Luhrmann's adaptation of *Romeo & Juliet* or Amy in the film *Bad Mums*, screaming in the car after the school drop off.

** These are ancient Greek swear words. I thought it was more interesting than screaming 'fuck' the first time and also good to start the play in the original language. So, first scream this very loudly and unthinkingly in ancient Greek and then 'fuck ... fuck'. I don't think just a scream would be as good as screamed swear words. I want this opening to be as shocking as a woman outside alone would have been to an all-male Greek audience. Antigone should be seen immediately as a rebel, as well as vulgar to many audience members. I think the swear words would add the shock value which an un-chaperoned woman no longer provokes for most modern-day audiences.

(approaches ANTIGONE)
What are you doing Tigi?! Tell me.
And then we've got to go
You know we're not allowed outside the palace gates
unchaperoned

ANTIGONE:
(beckoning then sitting down)
Please, Izzy. Stop
For once can you just sit down with me and talk
I can't cope with this alone

(looks up, calm now but distraught)
I really thought our luck was changing
Like finally, *finally*
after everything we've been through
the Gods might have noticed
we've done nothing wrong

I'm *not* dad
You're not mum
It's not our fault our family is so fucked up

*(stands up and announces it to the audience, very
theatrically, loud, as if drunk)*
Go on! Look at us!
Dirty Daughters of famous King Oedipus!
Fated Children of Incestuous Blood!
Sisters of the World's Worst Fucking Luck!
Mum fucks son fucks dad

10

(more upset than angry now)
Fuck!

(ISMENE pulls her down, looking around, highly anxious.
ANTIGONE continues but to her sister only now)

ANTIGONE:
(quieter, to ISMENE, laughing lightly)
And I know what you're gonna say already, Izzy
Oh Antigone! Calm down
Oh Antigone, life isn't easy!
Oh there goes Antigone, daydreaming again!
Well maybe I *am* dreaming
and maybe you're right
but I was *really* starting to believe things were getting
better this time

Wrong again, wasn't I?

(looking at ISMENE for a reaction, none, more animated again, then
ISMENE looks confused)

ANTIGONE:
(continues)
Izzy? Have you got nothing to say?

(Silence from ISMENE)

ANTIGONE:
(continues)
Ismene?

(louder)
Oh my Gods, do you not know?
Nothing?

Izzy! Do you not know that our Uncle, lord almighty
King Kreon
whatever we're supposed to call him now
has been strutting around the city all morning
proclaiming it to everyone?

(ISMENE is confused, shakes her head)

ANTIGONE:
(continues)
Do you really know nothing?

ISMENE:
(finally, shouting)

No, Tigi, I don't.
I haven't got a clue what you're talking about
What I *do* already know
is enough for me to deal with right now ok?

I know this;
that both our brothers are gone!
that the enemy has withdrawn;
that the two of us are completely and utterly alone now
that is *all* I know,
and I don't want to know any more

ANTIGONE:
You can't ignore this Izzy

Come closer
the city listens to everything

ISMENE:

I don't want to know, Tigi
please, you're making me panic again

ANTIGONE:
(quickening)
Good! You should be panicking
Everybody should be panicking

King Kreon has just announced the ruling
for both of our brothers
You have to know this Izzy
are you listening?

ISMENE:
(giving in sadly)
I'm listening

ANTIGONE:

Eteocles has been named a hero by the *King*
Defender of the city
Honoured with the most beautiful burial
fit for the God of Death beneath.
The underworld will welcome him kindly Izzy
Hades will be happy
and I'm so happy he will be

ISMENE:

He'll be at peace?

Yes, at peace.

(a moment of tenderness between ANTIGONE and ISMENE)

ISMENE:
(nervous)

And Polynices?

(pause)

ANTIGONE:

Polynices . . . is being punished . . .
with the worst sentence there is

Kreon's very first order as King was to declare him a traitor
He had the royal guards strip our little brother
first of his uniform; second of his underwear
bare as newborn breath, naked on the hilltop
for everyone to stare at

All by himself, Izzy, shamed and naked,
for everybody to see
as if he didn't die just as painfully as Eteocles,
just as slowly, just as young
as if his blood didn't water the soils of this city
just as sickly,
as if he didn't also die, as if he isn't also *dead*, Izzy

Not one single sprinkle of soil is allowed to glitter our
little brother's skin

14

A brand new law. Kreon just passed it. You *know* what
it means.

The Gods don't welcome anybody below without a
proper burial
and Kreon has made it clear that that can never be.

He's not allowing any funeral
All blessings have been banned
No tomb is being built
No wine is to be sipped
No crowds are allowed to gather
No songs can be sung
Not even family can visit him
Not even *us*

(ISMENE cries, ANTIGONE becomes less sympathetic, more agitated)

Don't cry Izzy! There's no point!
Tears are targeted too
Nobody is allowed to mourn him

(to herself)
His poor flesh, a landscape laid for a feast
glorious orchard of blood and skin
for crows and vultures and ravens
to swoop down upon

clink beak
peck bone
lick clean

spit pips

(looks up, serious, slower now)
and according to our new *King*,
this
is justice

You'll see the King soon enough, Iz
He's coming out of the palace now
to announce it 'officially'
Can't you already imagine him?
Prancing through the city gates
voice of fucking thunder
as if that golden piece of metal atop his skull
gives him some sort of Zeus-like powers
repeating Gods know how many times
what he's been spouting all morning already

'Nobody is to bury that boy.'
That boy.
As if he's suddenly forgotten his own nephew's name.

He's declared a public stoning as the punishment
for anyone who disobeys

A public stoning!
Why do we love such sick parades?
Everybody in the city betting on each blow
children clapping hands as rocks smash bone
battering long last death into another bloody victim
cheers erupting, spectators exchanging winnings;

screaming killings over salted snacks
It's so disgusting. We have to do something
I can't stand this any more Izzy

(to ISMENE)
So,
are you with me?

ISMENE:
*(wiping her eyes)**

What?

ANTIGONE:
Are you helping me or not?

ISMENE:

With what?

ANTIGONE:
With the body, Izzy?

ISMENE:

Antigone,
please tell me you're not thinking about burying your
brother yourself when you just told me
the penalty is death

---

* There are many dialogues like this in the play that are to be read as fairly quick-fire,
often rhyming discussions, back and forth without pause, the rhyme often connecting
the two characters' lines.

ANTIGONE:

He's *both* our brothers, Izzy
even if you wish he wasn't yours as well
I'm not letting him down

ISEMENE:

but Kreon has just announced—

ANTIGONE:

(interrupting)

I know what Kreon announced, I just told you myself!
If you ever actually listened to me
you might realise I don't care
what Kreon just declared
This is our family, Izzy
Some things are more important than following orders

Yes, Kreon is now King
But he's king of *one* city,
that doesn't give him the right
to decide our little brother's future
for the rest of fucking eternity!
Polynices needs to rest in peace Izzy

ISMENE:

*(trying to quiet ANTIGONE down, slowly
whispering this)*

Tigi, please, think properly
Have you forgotten how our parents died
because I certainly haven't!

Hated by everyone
Blinded by shame
Left to rot
in sullied graves

And now this
Our brothers both dead in one single day
Blood soaked simultaneously
into the same polluted ground

(crescendo)
Do we really need more trouble in our lives right now?
Have we not been through enough?

It's just the two of us left, Tigi, just *us*
and right now, we are both still breathing

Kreon is King. If we disobey his law
ours will be the most horrendous deaths of all.

Stones, Antigone! Stones will be thrown!
Have you actually felt the weight of one?

(lifts a stone)
Take it! Take it!
You know how much our leaders love
to throw these at disobedient women

Our bones will be broken one after the next,
those bets wagered on *our* final breaths –
do you really want the last sensation either of us suffer

to be our own skulls smashing broken pottery
as crowds stand waving flags above our bloody corpses
because I, sure as Hades hell, do not

Despite everything this world has thrown at us
Despite *all* the injustice
I *like living*

(breathless, slower)
Antigone –
we're *women*
We can't fight these men

and we are young and they are older
and stronger and richer
and they are *armed*

We have to follow their rules
no matter how hard

I'll beg the dead to forgive me
for even talking about this to you
but while I'm living with the living
I have to obey living laws

I know my place, Antigone.
You've got to learn yours.

(pause)

Tigi, did you hear me?

ANTIGONE:

(slow, tempered, creepy almost)

yes, Ismene[*]
you're right beside me
how could I not hear

we're done now anyway

I was wrong to ask you for help.
I thought you were different
but you're just as scared and selfish as the rest of them

If you begged to help me now, held out your open hand
I wouldn't hold it for a second

Do what you want; cry all you like
I'm not abandoning our little brother
and if I die, it must be my time to go

Hades will welcome me below
Both our brothers will be there waiting to embrace me
and I will run into their arms with my head held high

Obedience will always be the easiest option, Izzy
– that doesn't make it right[**]

---

[*] At this point, Antigone stops using nicknames for her sister so this use of the full 'Ismene' should be emphasised. In the original, the introduction by Antigone of her sister is a very strong, untranslatable use of Greek language – it has been previously translated as 'my sister Ismene'. I have used nicknames to try to mimic this familial closeness, which slowly diminishes throughout the play.
[**] Noam Chomsky quote

(slowly)

I want an easy life as much as you
I don't *want* to break laws
and if man's laws were *just*
I wouldn't have to

but right now, they are wrong
so I side with Justice
and I side with the Gods

Death is a much, much longer adventure than life
and when we're dead, the dead
will be the only friends we have
so it's them I'll worry about impressing

ISMENE:
(worked up)*
I don't *ignore* the Gods, Tigi,
but I've no power to fight the living

ANTIGONE:
Well enjoy your tears
I'm drying mine

I'll need to see clearly
to dig

---

* Again, this dialogue should be a fast-paced rhyming to and fro.

ISMENE:

please don't do this
I'm so worried about you

ANTIGONE:

It's yourself you should worry about

ISMENE:

I'll do that too, believe me, I will
and if you still go through with this

(takes ANTIGONE's hand)
I won't tell anybody
I promise

ANTIGONE:

What?

(pushes hand away)
You really don't get it, do you?

(slowly, loudly, sure)
I want you to tell everyone

I want you to scream it from the mountain's tip
so the great Thebes dragon might finally awaken
to all this injustice, unleash its wings
and tumble the city walls
with this law-breaking treachery

I want you to sweat this story out
until steam rises hot to the skies
till clouds' bellies burst with the
storm rains rivers flooding banks breaking
this *bloody silence*
let the floodgates open
let it seep into the city's water systems
for all citizens to swallow as they sip
till everybody feels it deep inside their stomachs
It's the silence I'm so sick of, Izzy
Silence changes nothing!

ISMENE:

Calm down, Antigone. You're burning

ANTIGONE:

The dead are cold. They'll welcome my heat

ISMENE:

If you manage to please them
which you won't

ANTIGONE:

You never know if you don't try

ISMENE:

That doesn't make it *right, Tigi*

ANTIGONE:

Says who?

ISMENE:

Me, and so many other people will too
Even attempting this is wrong

ANTIGONE:

Say that again
and I'll hate you even more than I do right now
Just go, leave me alone now
Death doesn't scare me half as much as silence*
Turn your cheek Ismene. Close your eyes tight
I'm *not* closing mine.

ISMENE:

It's not that simple, Tigi, and you know it
But I'll stop. I'm too tired to argue with you anymore

Do what you have to

(quietly, lovingly)
I'll be here
for you
and …
and I will still love you

CHORUS:
(very sudden interruption, singing a medley of the two songs 'Oh What a Beautiful Morning' and 'We are the Champions' in a celebration of Thebes' victory in the war)

---

* Martin Luther King quote

(after singing first two lines of the chorus of 'Oh What a Beautiful Morning'* change lyrics from third line of chorus onwards to the following)

> Look at the sun as it rises
> Triumphant (triumphant!)
> Victorious (victorious)
> Over Thebes' seven glorious gates!

(stop singing)

CHORUS 1:

We won!

CHORUS 2:

Oh it's brilliant, isn't it!

CHORUS 3:

I heard it was Zeus

CHORUS 1 AND 2:

Zeus?

CHORUS 3:

Yeah. Zeus did it.
Finished them off

(animated)
with a battering of thunder

---

* For copyright reasons, we cannot print the actual lyrics referred to so have offered instructions on which bits to sing from the original songs before the adaptations.

and a big blast of lightning
– apparently

CHORUS 7:
(imitating Zeus)
Me, Zeus, big brave God of Thunder
Raaaaahhhhhhhhh

CHORUS 6:
(pretending to be an enemy soldier)
Oh no, it's Zeus
quick, run

CHORUS 7:
(running after the soldier, hands out like guns)
Lightning strike
bam bam

CHORUS 6:
(does a fake death scene)

CHORUS 5:
Oh Zeus!

CHORUS 7:
Oh Hera, my Goddess
you're so hot right now

CHORUS 5:
Hotter than that other Goddess
I caught you with the other day

(start a fake argument)

CHORUS 4:

Stop!
People have died!
It's not funny!
Both the kings are dead
We shouldn't be celebrating

(pause, the rest of the CHORUS look a bit guilty, not sure how they feel)

CHORUS 2:

We still won!
We still defeated them!

CHORUS 1:

And there's a new king now
At least let us celebrate a little bit

(CHORUS mutter agreement)

(Rest of the CHORUS begin singing again, singing the first line of the chorus to 'We are the Champions' as it is and then adapting the following lines, as below. Only CHORUS 4 does not join in, huffing at the side)

The enemy soldiers have fled
We are the champions
Let's go out dancing
The temples are—

CHORUS 3:

Wait! Stop!

(sudden halt of the music)
(CHORUS starts whispering amongst themselves)

CHORUS 2:

Is . . . is that the new king? I'm sure it's him!

CHORUS 5:

What do we do?
Curtsy?

CHORUS 4:

I don't know how to curtsy

CHORUS 3 AND 5:
(demonstrating)

Like this

CHORUS 1:

Why's he here?

CHORUS 3:

Shhh!
Sit down

CHORUS 6:

No! Stand up!

(Enter KREON, swift change of mood. Silence as he enters)

(CHORUS all stand)

KREON:
(to the CHORUS)
Good afternoon, loyal citizens

(coughs, nervous, very rehearsed)
I am your new King. Please, sit.

Firstly, I would like to thank each and every one
of you for your tremendous support during these
turbulent times and ask that you join me in thanking
the Gods for helping sail our great city to safety. The
storm has finally passed. We are victorious it is true.
My condolences to all who have lost loved ones in this
bitter battle. Believe me when I say I mourn with and
for you.

As you know, I have only been your King for a short
time but in that short time I have seen so much cause
for hope. *You* are one of those. My people.

(CHORUS sit up straight, pleased with the compliment)

Citizens. Your obedience is outstanding.
It does not go unnoticed

First to King Laius, then Oedipus,
then his sons, Eteocles and Polynices

who, as most of you will know, are now dead

I was next in line and I am ready to prove myself.

(insincere again, clears throat, maybe moves to lectern to speak to audience and CHORUS, more like a political speech)

Our city is our ship and I assure you now
I will steer us to greatness again.

(most of the CHORUS stand up and cheer, clap; some don't)

Now, I imagine you're curious
to hear my decision concerning both previous kings.

I learnt of Eteocles' death yesterday with great
mourning
Brave soldier, loyal citizen, such a great, great man*
For this, I have made absolutely certain
every holy blessing will be present
The best tomb has been commissioned
Eteocles will be welcomed by Hades
with a hero's death, I have made sure of it

Some say it unwise to speak ill of the dead
but I think we may make an exception
for the *other* brother
(slight laughter as if an attempt at a joke)

---

* Trump is in my head here with the constant use of 'great' and 'greatness'.

This traitor, I'm sure you all remember
came storming back from exile thirsty for a fight
abandoning the Gods' trust, pulling us all into civil war
forcing innocent blood

*(getting more sure of his ideas now, but still a little as if
convincing himself)*
This other brother is enemy to every single one of us
and as an enemy, you *must* all agree
he does not deserve to rest in peace

This city, my city, is built only for good, law-abiding,
obedient men

(a bit more crazed)
He is not one of them

Yes! Traitors! Traitors deserve nothing more than to rot
butchered by birds for dogs to slather saliva over
cock leg up and piss upon

A traitor is *not* a hero, is he?
Death must *not* welcome him
What this traitor did
should never be forgotten*

People of Thebes, this is my decision

---

* think rhythm of gunpowder plot rhyme

CHORUS 1:

Do you agree with him?

CHORUS 3:
(laughing as if there's no option)

He's the King!

CHORUS 1:

What do you mean?

CHORUS 7:

Well, he's untouchable.
A king can't be wrong*

CHORUS 4:
(to KREON too)

When you're in charge
you can do anything you want.**

KREON:
*(happier, as if taking the advice,
realising his power)*

Yes, I can! I must!***

(back to business)

---

* This exchange in Greek by the Chorus would have had ominous undertones about auto-cratic rule. Mimicking Trump's line that 'you can do anything' when he sees a beautiful woman will hopefully remind modern audiences of this abuse of power in a similar way.
** Donald Trump quote on grabbing women, very similar to original text.
*** To me, this line is a turning point in Kreon becoming power hungry and more aggressive in his rulings.

As for you, my loyal, obedient citizens
we are relying on you all to keep watch

CHORUS:
(mumbling to one another)

All day?
Over the body?
We can't
What does he mean?
(to Chorus 5)
Go on ask him
(to Chorus 5)
Go on!

CHORUS 5:

OK!

CHORUS 5:
(stands up)

Pardon me, King.
Shouldn't other people keep watch?

KREON:

Not over the boy's body
I have guards for that!

CHORUS 1:

Then what are *we* watching for?

KREON:

Anything suspicious
Any talk about the boy

Any neighbours' whispers
Anybody you suspect might be disobeying my decision

CHORUS 4:
(to the others in the CHORUS)
Who would do that!

CHORUS 3:
(to KREON)
That would be suicide.

KREON:
Yes, but greedy men are easily bribed
not everybody shares your goodness

If you see anything at all
report it to the palace at once

(Enter GUARD, jumpy)

GUARD:
Excuse me, Sir, King, King Kreon, Great King Kreon
I won't say I ran here because I didn't
I kept stopping
Thinking, go back, Aleksander*
What are you doing?!
He'll have you for this
He will! King Kreon!
So I kept turning back in panic

---

* In the original this character has no name but I decided to add it to re-emphasise that we are still in Greece.

till my mind scolded again
Stop stopping, Aleksander!
You must tell the King!
And so I'd spin back round
all fluster, yes yes you must
the King will more likely
have your guts for garters*
if someone else tells him first

So in the end I came here
to tell you
even if I really,
really don't want to

(CHORUS all staring incredulously at the GUARD)
(KREON's response is obnoxious but maybe humorous)

KREON:

Pardon?

GUARD:

What? Right
I'll tell you then. King.

(breathes in, then exhales hard)
First,
it wasn't me
I didn't see who it was, so ...
there is no reason at all

---

* The language of the guard is poetic but clichéd.

that *I* should be punished?

For what?!

GUARD:
(to himself as much as anyone else)
Oh, it's bad

KREON:
(loses his temper)
I gather that, you koprìas*
Tell me

GUARD:

Yes, ok
so . . .

*(closes eyes then takes a few breaths very quickly,
very rushed, eyes closed until he's done)*
Somebody buried the body
Dug soil
Laid blessings

(starts to bow, and go)

KREON:

What?

---

* This is an ancient Greek insult about being dirty.

37

(slowly)
Which *man* has dared defy me *already*?

CHORUS:

GUARD:

Not me, King, not me
I would never do that
but I don't know who has

because you see,
there wasn't a scrap of evidence.

*(Silence. GUARD looks round, prolongs the silence as if making sure he
is permitted to continue to speak, then goes on)*

No pickaxe, I mean. No tracks
The person who did it left no trace
Footprints melted into snow

(excited)
Like a shadow fled!

(curbing excitement)
I mean, terrible

(Silence, awkward wait, no-one speaks)
(GUARD looks around again)

CHORUS:
(whispering to one another)
I'm not saying that!
You should

No you tell him

(to CHORUS 5)
You tell him
Go on

(CHORUS 5 walks up nervously to the King and taps him on the shoulder)

CHORUS 5:
Excuse me, King
We've had an inkling
that maybe, well

CHORUS 1:
(interrupts, excited, childlike)
Maybe the Gods did it!

KREON:
(laughing angrily at this suggestion)
The Gods!

CHORUS 1:
Yes!

CHORUS 5:
Well, maybe the Gods had *something* to do with it

KREON:
(slow, eerie)
An inkling you have?
That the Gods did this?

(raising his arms to the sky)
The Gods!
(screams)
Do you?

(CHORUS are silent)

KREON:
(continues)

You think the Gods have nothing better to do with
their holy time
than organise a burial for such a *loyal* citizen to this
city?
You think *the Gods* bother about this traitor's body?

You seem to be forgetting
within this little inkling of expert wisdom
that little invasion of this city during which
the honourable citizen you so speak of
came with an enemy army
to burn down the temples of
those Gods you are speaking of
I'll tell you all something now
and I advise you to listen
– You are wrong!

You want to know how this happened?
Ask me! I *know* how this happened!

It wasn't the Gods, you gràsons*
it was men! The same men whispering
ever since I took my rightful place as this city's King
Do you think I'm so stupid I don't hear them
conspiring another bloody rebellion
instead of obeying me?

It is not the Gods at play here, it is *greed*

I don't believe I even need to tell you this
because it is so blindingly obvious
A man has been bribed to do this

Nothing more evil than money has ever existed
The most worthy of citizens
agree to all manner of criminal scandal
for one sniff of riches

(to the GUARD, slowly, eerily)
Now *you*
listen to *me*

I swear by Zeus's thunder
if you do not uncover the man who did this
death will be the least of your worries

I will pin you down myself
until you confess what you did
clear and loud

---

* Ancient Greek insult for someone who smells like a goat

so every citizen sees
nothing is gained
(louder, hysterical almost)
from disobedience to the crown

GUARD:
*(panicking)**
May I please speak or just go now, sir?

KREON:
I'm done with your words!

GUARD:
Your mind or your ears, sir, which ones?

KREON:
What a ludicrous question!

GUARD:
Well, if it's your ears irritated
blame me for this
but if it's your mind
surely blame the man who did it

KREON:
Do you ever shut up?

---

* Another quick-fire back and forth rhyming dialogue with very short breath breaks
until the final line by Kreon 'I *will* find you guilty', which breaks the rhyme pattern.

GUARD:

I do
– when you see I'm innocent
I did nothing!

KREON:

But you did!
You did if I say you did!
I am King!

GUARD:

How terrible!
People with the power to judge,
judging like this!

KREON:

(very patronisingly, almost like talking to a child)
A philosopher now, are we? Very good!

(quickly and firmly)
Still, if you do not find the man who disobeyed me
I *will* find you guilty.

(Exit KREON)

(Exit GUARD)

CHORUS:
*(singing the first verse of 'What a Wonderful
World' but with 'we' replacing the 'I's and
changing the last line to the following)*

Oh the wonder of man!

Are those the right words?

Yeah! The wonder of man. That's the title of the whole song!

CHORUS:
*(continue, to the tune of the verse that begins:
'Oh the colours of the rainbow')*

Oh the birds – watch man snare!
Oh the fish – see man catch!
Oh the wild beasts – watch man tame
as they trot the mountain paths!
Oh the stallions and bulls
See the chains now round their necks!
Such resourceful skills has man
Genius man, whatever next?

(CHORUS stop)

CHORUS 6:
What's next? I can't remember the next verse

CHORUS 3:
(recites it like a poem, not singing)
How he steers the boats he builds
across the raging storms

How he ploughs each seeded field
till his palms are soaked in sweat
tilling drilling milling
everything that he can get,
we see . . .

(CHORUS back to singing enthusiastically)

CHORUS 5:
(happy)

trees of green

CHORUS 4:
(less sure)

deserts dry

CHORUS 7:

rising tides?

CHORUS 1:

melting ice?

CHORUS:

and we think to ourselves

(getting confused)

(CHORUS suddenly all jump back / scream. These lines are more like chattering, each chorus member taking on a different line)

Who's that?
It can't be!
It is, I'm sure
First the King
Now the princess
What's she doing?

(asks another CHORUS member)
Why are they dragging her like that?

CHORUS:
(more chattering now)
Do you think?
No! I don't think so
A girl?! She can't have
She'd need a lot of muscle

GUARD:
(trying not to smile too much)
No! Yes, I mean! Yes!
She did it!
We found her!
Where's the King?

(Kreon enters)

CHORUS 7:
Perfect timing!

What's so perfect about it?

GUARD:

Your highness. King.
I spoke too soon
To be honest
I swore I wouldn't come back
But I did

(slowly, celebratory)
She did it!
I swear to you on my dear mother's life
and I do love my mother dearly
We caught her
kneeling beside him
disobeying your rules
I came straight here to tell you

(an intricate bow, tries to leave)

KREON:

This ... girl?

(doesn't believe it)
Tell me how you found her *exactly*?*

---

* In this section, the Guard keeps trying to leave but Kreon keeps questioning him. Kreon's questions should always rhyme with the Guard's previous line, to increase the feeling that Fate won't let him leave.

GUARD:

Beside the boy, burying him.

(intricate bow again, quicker, and tries to run)

KREON:
(slowly)
Do you understand what you're claiming?

GUARD:
(excited almost)

I do.

KREON:

And you swear to me you're telling the truth?

GUARD:

Yes! The other guards saw her there!

(an intricate bow again and starts to run)

KREON:

How *exactly* did you *catch* her?

(GUARD breathes out slowly, resigned)

(The CHORUS's heads are all turned towards him)

GUARD:

I will *happily* tell you

*When the GUARD says this the CHORUS sit down and get comfy as if
they're kids about to listen to a story that they know is going to be a long one)*

GUARD:
*(pause, then quick storytelling,
very animated again)*
After your threats if you remember,
I returned to the hill myself
Swept the dust off the boy's body
Uncovered it fully again
like, like a traitor's body should be

Then we went, all us royal guards,
Aesop and Caesar, Hahn, Macario and me
back up that hill, upwind from the smell
I tell you for free there is no scent worse
than rotting flesh

and we watched
and we waited
and we waited there
and we waited more

*(CHORUS start to make faces because the story is taking too long,
maybe start to lean on each other's shoulders, lie back, close their eyes,
put blankets over the younger ones)*

GUARD:
(continues)

And it got so hot
glaring globe of sun

49

Gods, we were sweating

Then, out of nowhere
this dust storm started
Trees, shaken by the Gods
hurricane heat swirls above
clouds of smoke surrounding us
the entire sky coughing up;
a plague it was and us
dust choked, eyes burning
We *had* to shut them, King

and when we open them again
who do we see? *That* girl!

*(points finger, but then drops hand, looks a little sad,
speaks softer now)*
On the hill
scooping the last of the dry dust
scattering it across her brother's body
as she whispers blessings above him

We watch her mourn him
crying in defiance of your law

We've got her! we whisper
Rush in! Arrest! we scream
weapons ready for some sort of struggle
but

nothing

she just stands there
like she's expecting it

denies none of it
which, upsetting as it is
to see our princess in such a state,
is a relief for me
what with your threats
if I'm honest

KREON:
(to ANTIGONE)
Girl, do you *deny* this?

ANTIGONE:
(looks him in the eye)
No. I did it.

KREON:
(to the GUARD)
Go

(GUARD does the bow once more and legs it)

KREON:
(to ANTIGONE)
And you knew it was forbidden?

ANTIGONE:
The whole city knows it is forbidden

KREON:

So, you *chose* to break my law

ANTIGONE:

Yours. Yes
but not the Gods'

KREON:

The Gods'?

ANTIGONE:

The Gods'. Yes. I obey their laws, not yours.
Justice and Fate – I obey them. Zeus – I obey him.
Hera – I obey her. Aphrodite, Apollo, Ares, shall I
keep going?
Gaia, Goddess of our Earth, oldest Goddess, Goddess
of everything
– I obey her. Goddess of Fertility,
of birth of life of living.
And Hades – Oh Hades! I obey him!
Hades, God of dying! God of dust! God of blessings!
God of being allowed to cover your little brother's
bloody naked body
when the King decides it right to punish him even after
he is dead
– yes, I obey Hades not you
not the paper-thin scribbles you claim I have to respect
because you wrote them whilst balancing a golden hat
on your skull

Kill me if you must, Uncle
you have *no idea* how it feels
to watch someone you love rot in open air
because of one man's fickle laws

I'm not frightened of death anymore
and I'm not afraid of men like you
I've been to the hilltop
I've done what I *had* to do
and if you still see me as some foolish little girl
perhaps it takes one to know one, old fool

Death will be a welcome break
when life is pain and misery

Do what you want with me, Kreon
(slowly, dramatically, to Kreon directly)
but I have a name
My name is Antigone

(CHORUS gasp)

CHORUS 6:
Did you hear what she just said to the *king*?

CHORUS 1:
(whispers)

That was amazing

CHORUS 3:

It was stupid!

Did you see his face?!

I wonder what he'll do? Oh Gods

(as if to stop the chatter of the CHORUS)

No need to wonder
Let me enlighten you all

(matter of fact)
This girl knew the law and broke the law. *Twice.*
Now she struts boasting about her crimes
as if she knows better than a King
Yes, she is my niece, my kin, a princess, that is irrelevant
Family must never come before government
A law breaker is a law breaker
and a law breaker must be punished
If not, what's the use of making bloody laws!
Tell me what the city will think of me if I don't punish her?
That *I* am the little girl and that *she* has the balls!

(turns quickly to ANTIGONE, keeps the pace)
Let me tell *you* something now, *young girl.*
A conceited criminal is the most shameful thing alive

(calm now)

So kill me.
The people are on my side

KREON:
(to the public/CHORUS, theatrically)
Well that proves it. This girl has lost her mind

(to ANTIGONE)
Nobody is on your side.
The citizens are overwhelmingly in support of the
punishment
more support in fact than any King before me has
ever won
They have been telling me in person

ANTIGONE:
I've lost my mind! Yet it's you who really believes
people speak their truth with your sword two inches
from their tongues

KREON:
Aren't you ashamed of what you've done?

ANTIGONE:
*(slow, angry, calm, almost exasperated
to be asked again)*
I buried a brother I love

KREON:
Who killed your other brother

ANTIGONE:
I know what happened

KREON:

So you're happy to love a murderer?

ANTIGONE:

Two kings in battle

KREON:

One defending, the other attacking our city

ANTIGONE:

The Gods see it differently

KREON:

Oh please. Alive or dead
nobody wants evil laid beside them

ANTIGONE:

Polynices was *not* an evil person

KREON:

Corruption is corruption

ANTIGONE:

And hate is hate
and hate achieves nothing
I chose love, Kreon. Love!

KREON:

Choose bloody love then!
I'm sure Hades will give you a hand searching for it
in the scrapyards of hell

I'm not wasting any more of my time arguing with
a girl!

(to the GUARD, screaming, mistakenly sure of himself)
Where's the sister? It's so obvious she helped as well!
Bring her out!

CHORUS 3:

Ismene!

CHORUS 4:

Oh – look at her! Her face is all blotchy

CHORUS 1:

Do you think she's been crying again?

KREON:

Of course she has
they're all brilliant at that, aren't they?
Crying, for pity's sake
here she comes, second snaky slut

(to ISMENE)
So. Humour me.
Or are you planning to deny your part in all this?

*(I imagine the CHORUS sitting between ANTIGONE and ISMENE
for this argument. CHORUS centre stage. Characters left and right.
Maybe CHORUS cross-legged sitting down in a group on a mat, again
a little like in a school, their backs to the audience so they almost become
the audience and the audience become the chorus; the heads of the*

chorus turning to each character as they speak their lines, much like the audience is likely to do)

ISMENE:

I don't, King. I helped my sister

ANTIGONE:

(starts to run at her, GUARD holds her back)
You liar! You did nothing
and you know it!

ISMENE:

Antigone, I'm here
to share the shame

ANTIGONE:

No, Ismene
You can*not* have this both ways
First, you walk away from me
then come back to claim the credit
Look at my hands! Blistered!
Covered in blood!
Let me see your scars?
Let me see!

ISMENE:

Tigi, please

ANTIGONE:

Don't please Tigi me
Tell them the truth
and walk free

ISMENE:

But, you and me, remember
Your fate is my fate

ANTIGONE:

We were children, Ismene
it's a bit late for that now

ISMENE:

But I can't live without you

ANTIGONE:

I'm sure you'll find a way

ISMENE:

But everything we've been through together

ANTIGONE:

Together?! Together?! It's hardly the same!
I sacrificed all light the minute I decided to scatter soil!

ISMENE:

but you're my sister – I love you!

KREON:

Girls, girls, girls
Each bitch as hysterical as the next
One born that way
the other a recent convert it seems

(Now KREON takes the place of ANTIGONE, and CHORUS continue watching the arguments as if a tennis match)

ISMENE:

Trauma traumatises people, King
It's hard not to be emotional

KREON:

Yes, that happens when you help criminals

ISMENE:

She's my sister

KREON:

She's done with. Forget her

ISMENE:

But—

(as if grappling for arguments)
your son?

KREON:

What about him?

ISMENE:

Haemon. He loves her

KREON:

Love! There are plenty more fields my son can hoe

ISMENE:

But you know
he *loves* Antigone

KREON:

My son will *not* marry an enemy

ISMENE:

But the wedding is agreed

KREON:

And the bride is no longer fit for service

ISMENE:

So you'll steal his dream

KREON:

Death will steal it, not me

(CHORUS join in the back and forth)

CHORUS 5:

So the sentence is set?

CHORUS 1:
(to the others)

Will Antigone really die?

KREON:

Yes! Of course she will
I've been given no choice
Does nobody see that?!

Guards!

Take this sister in
Do not let either of them out of your sight
They might be brave enough to break my laws
but even the bravest rebels flee when death bites

CHORUS:
(chatting, solemn)

CHORUS 1:

Poor Antigone

CHORUS 3:

Poor Ismene! She didn't do *anything*

CHORUS 4:

Well, why doesn't she just say that?

CHORUS 3:

You try having the childhood they had

CHORUS 2:

My dad says that a family's curse is never broken

CHORUS 4:

It's nothing to do with that!
Stop making excuses for her –
Did you hear how she was talking to the King?

CHORUS 2:

Ismene?

CHORUS 4:

No! Antigone. She's so rude

CHORUS 7:

And she broke the law

CHORUS 4:

She knew what she was doing

CHORUS 3:

It was for her family!
Wouldn't you do that for me?

CHORUS 1:

I think she's the bravest princess I've ever seen!

CHORUS 4:

And how many others have you seen?

CHORUS 5:

Stop fighting!
Haemon's coming

CHORUS 1:

Is he crying too?

CHORUS 5:
(peering)

I can't see

KREON:
(to the CHORUS)

I guess we'll know soon enough

(HAEMON approaches)

KREON:
(to HAEMON)

Son, I presume you've heard my decision.
Do you see reason
or have you come to hound your poor father?

(pause)

HAEMON:

I see reason, sir
No marriage is as important
as supporting one's parents

KREON:
(smiling slightly, secretly relieved)

Good boy. I didn't doubt you for a second
Why do we have sons if not to back us up in battle?

Sit down, listen for a minute will you?
Let me tell you a thing or two about women
because *I know* women. I've seen them
manipulate men with the twitch of an eye*

---

* Donald Trump quote

Haemon, forget this bride of yours
She's not worth the trouble
No woman is
Least of all a criminal

I know she might feel like everything right now
I've been there many times but believe me, son,
that feeling fades just as quickly
That twitching in your groin will soon find another
target
and once that deed is passed, once relief has come
coldness quickly returns and then what are you left
with?
A lifetime chained to a frigid, greedy woman

(HAEMON looks sad, but trying to cover it)

KREON:
(continues, very slightly softer)

I have to do this, you understand, Haemon?
The girl broke the law.
A law the people of this city believe in.
Without punishment, law is nothing.
Some words of wisdom for you. Listen to me, son.
If you have to lose at anything in life, *never* lose to a
woman

And she, this one,
she disobeyed me like no other citizen has
How feeble I would seem – Think what would happen
if I gave in? Eased my laws now? The first law I made!

What would people think of me?
Flitting between opinions?
That I'm a liar? A weakling?
Men who cannot control their women surely cannot
run a city
I'd certainly be no king!

This is for the city's sake, son, not mine.
This is for justice.

The girl laughed at my laws. The girl laughed at us all.
The girl must be punished.

CHORUS 6:

Maybe he's right

CHORUS 4:

Shush, I think Haemon's replying

HAEMON:

I understand, father. I do
I would never say you're wrong
(light, nervous laughter)
I wouldn't know how to*
but, there *is* a slightly different opinion going round

Some say, the people
they're a bit intimidated perhaps
to tell you what they really think

---

* I think there's a little humour in this line.

It seems they sing
quite a different tune
amongst themselves

Those puddles lining city streets
reflecting moonlit chatter
well, there's a rumour

they fill with *tears, father,*
for her

(pace picks up, obviously in awe of / in love with ANTIGONE and this
shows gradually)

People *do* sympathise
Some go further, many in fact
are calling her defiance glorious

Of all citizens of this city
some say she deserves death *least*
that she is being punished unfairly

This chatter is firelit, father
and it is spreading as we speak
lover to lover, mother to child

children singing skipping rope rhymes
about her defiance of authority
her love for family

fending bite of dog and peck of bird
I heard the words 'first female knight'
the other night

women are whispering in awe across washing lines
gossiping in brothels; drunk men sing her name
in taverns into goblets, it's blazing to a tragedy

Father, I've heard the sobs myself
the city *is* weeping
there *is* love for ... this ... rebel

(change of tone, realising he got carried away)
Now, believe me
nothing is more important than your success, father
which is exactly why I'm thinking

(slowing down)
a compromise might be in order?
For your sake, I mean.

(KREON is silent, his reaction hard to read)

(HAEMON tries to keep arguing his case)

HAEMON:
The Gods do bless us with incredible brains
Of course, *you* are proof of that
But surely education is one of our greatest blessings too

Listening to the latest news isn't weak, father
Nobody will laugh at you for taking advice
In fact, the man who will not change his mind

who states his opinions as if they are fact
when in fact they are merely his opinion
that is the man most likely laughed at in the end

(Silence from KREON)

(HAEMON looks around nervously but continues, as if he's just thought of this new metaphor)

HAEMON:
(continues)

In Winter! Think!
When the Gods blow the bitterest storms
isn't it the trees that bend trunks to the breeze a bit
that overcome

whilst those stubborn standing straight
refusing to budge
most likely snap?

(pause, panics a bit at KREON's lack of reaction)
I'm younger, I know that
and you are much, much cleverer than I am
and if I had one wish we would all be born with perfect
wisdom

but we're not

Not even Kings

CHORUS 5:

I agree with Haemon

CHORUS 7:

Maybe they'll learn from each other

(KREON immediately negates the CHORUS's hope)

KREON:

So, rulers are supposed to listen to the youth now, are
they?

HAEMON:

*(breathes out with the frustration that his speech did
nothing)*
No, father,
not if the youth, as you call us, are wrong
but if the youth have reason, why does age matter?

KREON:

You realise you're standing up for a traitor?

HAEMON:

I can't stand traitors

KREON:

and her?

HAEMON:
(adamant)

The people disagree

KREON:

So now I should listen to what the people *and* the
youth tell me?

HAEMON:

Can you hear yourself? How ancient do you sound?

KREON:

Ancient enough to own a city!

HAEMON:
(starting to lighten up a bit, grow in confidence)
You don't own it, you rule it!

KREON:

Last time I checked, it belonged to its ruler

HAEMON:

Try ruling it with no citizens!

KREON:
(to the CHORUS)
Seems this boy is siding with the women

HAEMON:

It's you I'm trying to help, not them

KREON:

By disobeying me?

HAEMON:

I don't disobey you, father, I simply disagree.
There's a big difference

KREON:

And my God-given authority?
You disagree with that then?

HAEMON:

With you *mis*-using it *against* the Gods. Yes!

KREON:

This is worse than I thought!
Someone help my son!
He's even weaker than a woman
I've birthed a little cunt

HAEMON:

I'm not a ... as you said ... father
and I will not ignore
this injustice any longer

KREON:

This isn't about justice!
This is about her!

HAEMON:

This is about what is right!

KREON:

You will never marry her alive!

HAEMON:

Then she'll die, and more deaths will follow,
I assure you!
And they will be your doing!

KREON:

You threaten me now?

HAEMON:

I don't threaten you
I simply speak my mind

KREON:

And what a mind it is!
Infatuated with a traitor
Disobedient to a King
You should be ashamed of yourself

HAEMON:

And you should try listening
to someone else for once
because despite your finest fantasies, father
you do not know everything

KREON:

I am king!

HAEMON:

Yes, one who vastly overestimates
his own intelligence it seems

KREON:

I demand silence from a son!

HAEMON:

Demand silence all you like
Unfortunately shutting up the opposition
still does not make you right

KREON:

(overly emotional, as if that was the last straw)
Guards, find the girl!
My son would like to watch her die

HAEMON:

(slower, calm, in contrast to KREON's rage)
Is this how desperate you are now, you sad old man
We're done here

CHORUS 5:

Where's he going?

CHORUS 4:

I don't know, he just ran off

CHORUS 2:

Where to?

KREON:

Who cares
Let him go
I've got women to kill

CHORUS 5:

(shocked, worried even)

Both?!

KREON:

(pretending he changes his mind totally of his own will)
Yes! No, I mean, of course, just one of them
Just one lifted a finger

CHORUS 1:

(steps forward, curious but blunt, quiet)
How? How will you do it?

KREON:

(slowly, calm)
Soon. Tonight. At sunset.
The guards will take her
to a cave up past the hill
I found it myself. A perfect spot
One single crack of light
A little water, bread and cheese to eat
Then left alone to rot
A boulder will seal the exit shut

CHORUS 1:
Cheese? I thought the punishment was death?

KREON:

Yes, it is
A death sentence is undoubtedly the correct decision

CHORUS 1:

Then why are you leaving food in the cave?

KREON:

Because, because

(slightly stumbling)
I have decided
to avoid a *direct* execution in this case
just to make 100% certain we do not incur
any ridiculous unnecessary Godly pollution

That way, the girl can pray all the breath she has
for Hades and Zeus and Gaia to rescue her
until she finally realises what good it does anyone
to beg the Gods for mercy while they disobey the King

Either way, this way,
when she does die
and she will die
our hands will be perfectly clean

CHORUS:

(Maybe: As the CHORUS sing, HAEMON and ANTIGONE or two figures representing them are sitting kissing and giggling and stroking hair, staring at each other's faces etc. for the length of this chorus. Not

as part of the actual story, but as an example of the delights of Eros and also to allow some heat into the play and to allow the audience to see these two together and increase sympathy for them after this moment.

or

HAEMON and ANTIGONE dance together to the songs)

CHORUS 1:[*]

I feel sick
Where's Haemon gone?

CHORUS 4:

I don't know

CHORUS 1:

Do you think she'll die?

CHORUS 5:

I don't know

CHORUS 1:

Do you think he went to save her?

CHORUS 5:

I don't know!

---

[*] Throughout this, CHORUS 1 is extremely confused and the other chorus members are sort of excited, agitated, giggling around her.

CHORUS 1:
Then why was he running so fast?

CHORUS 7:
Eros I think

CHORUS 1:
What?

CHORUS 7:
Eros – Love!

CHORUS 1:
What's Eros love?

CHORUS 5:
You'll understand when you're older

CHORUS 1:
I hate it when people say that. Just tell me

CHORUS 5:
It's Eros
God of passion
Everyone in the world's obsessed with him

(CHORUS 1 just looks confused)

CHORUS 3:
(gets up, dramatically)

Eros

God of lusting
God of love

What's lust?

You'll learn when you're older!

Oh shut up!

(REST OF CHORUS sing excerpt from Sam Cooke, 'Cupid')

Who's Cupid? What are you all talking about?

(gets up too)

Eros!
God of kissing
God of touching
God of yum

What do you mean touching?

(CHORUS sing chorus of 'I Touch Myself')

Like tickling?

CHORUS 5:

Sort of

CHORUS 1:

Like an itch?

CHORUS 5:

A bit!

CHORUS 1:

Like a cuddle?

CHORUS 5:

A bit!

CHORUS 1:

Like friendship?

CHORUS 5:

No, that's Philia love
This is Eros love

CHORUS 4:

Hot!
Blood love!

CHORUS 1:

Blood?
Like family love?

CHORUS 3:

No! that's Storge love
it's not *because* of blood
It's *in* your blood
It sends your blood
to parts of your body
you didn't feel blood in before
until you swell swarms of love
until you want to explode

CHORUS 1:

Like your heart?

CHORUS 5:

Not quite!

CHORUS 1:

Your eyes?

CHORUS 3:

Well ...

CHORUS 4:

More like your fingers

CHORUS 5:

And your phallus

CHORUS 3:

If you have one!

CHORUS 6:

Well your vulva!

CHORUS 2:

And your tongue!
and your toes!

CHORUS 1:

Your toes?
What have toes got to do with love?!

(CHORUS except CHORUS 1 fall, giggling, singing chorus lines from 'Please Me' while still on the ground)

CHORUS 1:

So is Eros why Haemon was shouting?

CHORUS 7:

Yes! because he wants Antigone

CHORUS 1:

To marry?

CHORUS 2:

Yes! And to kiss!

CHORUS 4:

And to consummate with!

CHORUS 7:

And he's losing his mind at the thought of losing her!

(CHORUS except CHORUS 1 sing first two lines of 'How Do I Live Without You')

CHORUS 1:

Aren't there other people he can marry?

CHORUS 5:

It's not that simple!
He wants her!

(CHORUS except CHORUS 1 sing final lines from 'I Have Nothing')

CHORUS 1:

Oh, I think I'm feeling something
it feels like an energy
a rushing

(CHORUS except CHORUS 1 sing chorus lines from Gabrielle Aplin's 'The Power of Love')

(CHORUS quieten, stop and turn as ANTIGONE enters)

ANTIGONE:

Why have you all stopped?

I'm about to be left in a stone-cold grave
still breathing living breath
too dead for the living
too alive for the dead
and the whole city is suddenly silent?

Why is nobody crying for me anymore?

Everybody's rushed back into their houses
Even the river seems to be running away
Just the flowers face me
(no response) Is this death already?
Is this how it is? Just silence?
Just the backs of people's heads
pretending to see nothing?

No, no, there is something!
Oh the sun! The sun still kisses my skin
I'll close my eyes and savour it
Keep singing, please. What was the song?
The melody was so sweet

(CHORUS stay silent)

ANTIGONE:

I said keep singing, please
Why won't you sing for me?
What have I done?

CHORUS 4:

You broke the law

CHORUS 3:

And argued with the King

CHORUS 2:

We're not meant to argue with Kings

84

CHORUS 1:

But

ANTIGONE:

But?

CHORUS 1:
I still think it was good, what you did

CHORUS 5:
Kings hate disobedience

CHORUS 1:
Maybe *Kings* should learn to listen

CHORUS 5:
Be quiet, people might hear

CHORUS 3:
And she shouldn't break the law

CHORUS 1:
Maybe Kings shouldn't make bad laws

CHORUS 4:
Maybe she never stood a chance

CHORUS 5:
You can't *still* blame it on her childhood
Kreon doesn't listen
but she doesn't really listen either

It's her actions that are the problem;
her attitude, her temper

ANTIGONE:

You're right! You're right again!
I am as stubborn as the rest of them
It runs in my blood
Haemon could never have loved me
I was so stupid to think he could

CHORUS 4:

It could be much worse
At least you're not being killed

CHORUS 6:

Or dying in battle

CHORUS 3:

Or battling disease

CHORUS 1:

You still have a chance
to live, I mean
I think Hades will help you

ANTIGONE:

Do you?

(looks up, notices the sky)
I'm not so sure anymore

If Hades was on my side
why is the light fading already?
Sunset, they said, *sunset* they'd come for me

but the sun is already setting
too early; I can see
the moon swaps places with it fast

the first star of night
already glitters in the black
If Hades doesn't want me yet

why doesn't he hold back
the cresting moon?
Soak the sunset's flame-lit fury?

How can the God of Light
still burn so beautifully
when all this is happening to me?

KREON:

Yes, yes, very pretty.
Everybody would try their hand at poetry before death
if it did any good
but it doesn't

(to the GUARD, as if reciting a mock poem)
Oh moon! Oh sky! Oh guards! It's time!

I've important matters to attend to
Take the prisoner to the cave
Let Fate decide the rest

(KREON starts to leave and then turns)

KREON:

Forgive me. I forget

(formally, sarcastically)
Does the criminal have any last words to honour us
with?

ANTIGONE:

No.

*(CHORUS turn to listen. CHORUS 1 steps towards ANTIGONE,
as if desperate for ANTIGONE to say something. ANTIGONE looks
down at CHORUS 1)*

ANTIGONE:
(continues)

Yes, sorry. Yes, I do.

*(ANTIGONE pauses to think, looking around until settling on a
thought. She kneels to CHORUS 1,* takes her hand, speaks this directly
to her, not the audience)***

When I was little, I had a list in my head of all the
things I would do one day. I found a ladder when I was
about your age, you see, and sneaked a peek over the

---

* depending on the height difference of the actors.
** Here, I have added more modern references to Antigone's 'future plans'. In the orig-
inal it focuses on marriage and having children. I haven't taken this out fully, as it is of
course still a goal of many, but I have added more to the speech for modern sympathies.

city walls. I was caught and scolded of course but the view in the distance was incredible. The whole world is out there and I wasn't allowed to see any of it.

When I am older, I thought, I, we, will be allowed. And when we are, I will be the first girl to run through those gates. I started daydreaming that day and I never stopped. I couldn't!

I imagined everything: walking through forests; sitting by the sea; sailing ships, maybe *our* hands at the wheels, *us* steering cities through storms.

I imagined a day us girls might be allowed to learn! To grab dusty books from the library shelves too; and to read and to write; to write our *own* stories and poems and speeches in our own ink on our own papyrus pads with our own hands and truths; and when we could, I would go straight to Thebes library and I would learn to read every page they let me flick through and then I'd read them all again and again and again until my eyes couldn't hold themselves open any longer; and then I'd dream of all the things I'd read.

And I would do so many other things as well. Walk outside alone or go and watch a play and drink heavy red wine from a big bubbling goblet in a theatre and I'd stand up and clap so loudly when the chorus finished singing, and afterwards I'd march to a tavern with my friends and I would take my own coins from my own purse and I'd buy salted fish and fruits and bread and lots and lots of honey for all of us and I'd eat it and let it drip down my chin and it would be so delicious, I could almost taste it already.

I imagined other things too: my glorious wedding, my glorious wedding night. Oh I've had a kiss you know and kissing is really nice but Haemon's skin on mine, oh Eros

(both giggle a bit at this)

I wanted to feel it all. And then, perhaps, me and Haemon, I thought, one day might have a baby, and then, if I put all of my daydreams together I imagined myself one day as the luckiest mother in Greece; able to pick up a book myself and read it line by line to my laughing child on a patch of grass together *outside* the city walls watching the stars spill the night with our secrets without anybody telling us to stop or act decent or go inside or be quiet or know our place because our place would be everywhere. Can you imagine, just imagine being able to read a book to your baby one day!

And we are *so* close. I can feel the seas change.

(almost a whisper, a bit sadder)
And even if it's too late for me, you still have a chance!

(more serious now, maybe closer to the girl)
So promise me ok, that when the day comes and they

open up the city gates to you, and the schools and
the theatres and all the libraries, that you will run out
straight away and choose the biggest book and see the
rudest play and write the best stories about all of your
adventures.

(CHORUS 1 smiles a little)

ANTIGONE:
(continues)

You promise?

*(CHORUS 1 smiles and nods; CHORUS 5 takes her away. ANTIGONE
turns, speaking more to herself now, as if able to stop putting on a happy
face for the young girl)*

ANTIGONE:

Perhaps death will be like birth
So maybe I will experience at least one of the things
I dreamt of
Perhaps it's just a different sort of push
So intense it screams the life from your bones

I don't know. Maybe that's how death is

(sadder)
Or perhaps it's not like that at all
Perhaps it's like pushing life from your bones
bones from your flesh, flesh from your skin
until there's nothing left of you
and then nothing and then nothing

and then nothing again
– what if that's death?

Just nothing

An empty cave where nobody is listening
where nobody is waiting, or
even if they are waiting, what if the faces of the dead
are so distorted, shadow mosaics of the faces
you used to love, that when death comes
it makes no difference because nobody
recognises anyone. What if that's death?
What if that's death? Just loneliness upon loneliness.
Just strangers. Just strangeness. Just silence
for the rest of time?

How can one single man
have so much power over my life?

(breathes again and turns to CHORUS)
Oh Gods, maybe Kreon *is* right
and if he is, if the Gods really agree
that burying my blood, my sweet young brother
if my loving was a holy sin,
then I promise I will suffer the punishment gladly

but if he *(points to Kreon)* is wrong!
If the Gods do not hate me
then all I beg is that he is punished like me

KREON:

That's quite enough

ANTIGONE:

(eyes closed in prayer, whispering, unheard)

KREON:

Praying can't help you now
Time is up

ANTIGONE:

(stands up, starts to walk)

Why are you all covering your eyes?
Surely I deserve more than that?
Stop it! Stop looking away!
Stop pretending you can't see this!
Look at my face!

Look at my face!

(pause, slower)
Now look at *them*
Don't ever forget what they've done

CHORUS 3:

I feel like I've heard this all before

CHORUS 5:

Me too

CHORUS 2:

Girl gets sent away
Locked out of the light
I've heard it so many times
the storyline never seems to change

CHORUS 1:

What do you mean?

CHORUS 3:

Rapunzel?

CHORUS 1:

Who's Rapunzel?

CHORUS 3:

A princess, like Antigone

CHORUS 5:

who paid for her family's past mistakes

CHORUS 1:

What happened?

CHORUS 3:

Well, she was locked up by a witch

CHORUS 1:

In a cave?

CHORUS 3:

No, in a tower. It's not *exactly* the same

CHORUS 1:

Did her mum and dad find out they were mother and son, like Oedipus and Jocasta?

CHORUS 3:

No, they stole lettuces

CHORUS 1:

That doesn't sound so bad

CHORUS 3:

From a witch's garden. She caught them and made them promise to give her their baby when she was born. Then she locked the baby in a tower.

CHORUS 1:

Did she die? The baby?

CHORUS 3:

No, she grew up and eventually a prince came to save her

CHORUS 1:

Like Haemon!

CHORUS 3:

Maybe, yeah

CHORUS 1:

Maybe Haemon will save Antigone?
Did the prince save Rapunzel?

CHORUS 3:

Erm, well . . .

CHORUS 1:

Well?

CHORUS 3:

He fell in love with her. And he tried to save her

CHORUS 1:

How?

CHORUS 3:

By climbing up her hair

CHORUS 1:

Her hair?

CHORUS 3:

It was really long

CHORUS 1:

Ok, then what? Did he save her?

CHORUS 3:
(dramatic storytelling)
Well, he tried, but Fate had other plans, and in a

twist of fortune the two lovers were caught by the
witch who tricked the prince into falling from
the tower, his eyes torn by thorns, the young
lovers banished to the desert where Rapunzel
gave birth and the blind prince spent eternity
trying to find her

CHORUS 1:

Oh, that's disappointing
Are there any with a better ending?

CHORUS 4:

The little mermaid?

CHORUS 7:

Voice is nicked by a witch, family abandon her?

CHORUS 2:

Little red riding hood?

CHORUS 7:

Are you kidding?

CHORUS 3:

Sleeping Beauty?

CHORUS 7:

Cursed by a bad fairy to be locked into sleep for
a hundred years, kissed by a prince bleeding from
battling thorns who she then has to marry. Maybe it
works out alright. Not sure.

CHORUS 2:

Snow White?

CHORUS 7:

Who's the fairest of them all? Stepmum wants to kill her because she's too pretty and pale. Married off to a prince who kisses her without asking when she's unconscious?

CHORUS 1:

Again?

CHORUS 7:

They all do it

CHORUS 1:

Haemon doesn't

CHORUS 7:
(smiles at CHORUS 1)
No, you're right. Haemon doesn't

(silence)

CHORUS 1:

Well, what about Antigone then?

CHORUS 7:

What?

CHORUS 1:

What about Antigone?
We don't know how that ends yet.
Maybe that'll be a better ending?

CHORUS 4:

With lots of kissing?

CHORUS 1:

Yes, lots of kissing! But maybe when the princess is
actually awake!

CHORUS 7:
(more positive)

Look, here's Tiresias. They always know what's going to
happen

(Enter TIRESIAS)

TIRESIAS:
(to KREON)

My lord

(to the CHORUS)
People of Thebes

KREON:
*(relieved and cheerier now ANTIGONE
is 'sorted')*

Tiresias! What news have you brought us this time?

TIRESIAS:

News you need to listen to

KREON:

Don't I always listen to you?!

TIRESIAS:

And the city survives because of it

KREON:

I owe you a lot, I know

TIRESIAS:

Well, listen now
Fate is rising
A flood is coming

KREON:

What on earth do you mean?

TIRESIAS:

I went to the forest today, Kreon
Watched the birds as I always do
The future is written in their flights

Today, there was no pattern in the skies
The birds did not flock together
but scattered across the air like storm

There was no song
Instead, screaming circling my head

beaks screeching like grief

They had no interest in the seeds
Do you know why?
Because, Kreon, they were eating each other

Bird biting bird, ripping feasting flesh
Murder is in the skies
Red raindrops drip madness!

Animals sense more than us,
Kreon
It is time to panic

I tried to stop it. I tried to calm the chaos
I lit all the altars;
laid the best cow carcasses as sacrifice
for every one of the Gods, but it would not stop

The God of Storm Winds raged
The Goddess of Frenzy and Rage paid no heed
The God of Fire refused to glow.
Not one single flame lit

Instead, thick slime slipped from the legs of the
carcasses.
The gall spat back. Bladder leaked into air. Fat flooded
the embers.
The candle wick covered till all attempt at fire was
useless

At first, I thought it was only *our* altar, but it wasn't,
it's all across the city, Kreon; in every temple
flames are being smothered by thick slime

The whole city is smoking. Nothing I do is working
The Gods are closed to prayer
The birds are screeching murder

I cannot decipher them anymore
The sacrifices failed, Kreon
They have *never* failed before

The Gods must be furious with you
Nothing makes sense
This city is sickened by your arrogance

Think very carefully about this
Everybody makes mistakes
but the man who refuses to change his mind
when all evidence is against him
is the most dangerous man there is

Admit your failings, Kreon
Stop turning your sword in the young boy's chest
He cannot bleed any more than he already has
He is already dead.

I care for this city and I care for you
My advice is good – take it

(very long silence to build the tension of what KREON will say – the CHORUS are waiting)

KREON:

I see
I see very clearly, thank you
I had a feeling about this. *(pause)*

(to TIRESIUS)
Your kind have lied so many times before.
So-called fortune tellers, and now here you are
trying to convince me that animals can feel what's
happening?
That birds too know more than Kings!
For the love of Gods, this is utterly ridiculous!

You are nothing but a moneyman
and I'm not your bloody merchandise

You must think I am so stupid
that I can't see you've taken a bribe
trying to tell me the Gods are against me
because a few birds are fighting

My decision was the right one
and my mind is not for changing

Let Zeus send his eagles
to rip bits of the boy's skin off,
scoff the flesh himself for all I care

and shit the body dropping by dropping
all across this Godforsaken city.*

How many times do I have to repeat myself
to you people:
The boy will not be buried!

TIRESIAS:

Can't you see?

KREON:

What am I meant to be seeing?

TIRESIAS:

That my prediction is life-saving

KREON:

And stupidity the most dangerous disease going

TIRESIAS:

A disease you appear gravely inflicted with

KREON:

I will not start arguments with a seer

TIRESIAS:

You started one the moment you accused me of
being a liar

---

* In the original, this line is blasphemous, so adding 'Godforsaken' emphasises this.

KREON:

Oh please, all you so-called fortune tellers bow down to
money

TIRESIAS:

I've heard the same thing about rulers

KREON:

You're talking to your King!

TIRESIAS:

A King whose city I've helped save
on several occasions
with my ridiculous predictions

KREON:

That doesn't make *this one*
true

TIRESIAS:

The future frightens me, Kreon
It should frighten you too

(slowly and carefully)
The Gods are mad with you
The sky sings with their spit
You cannot see it
But I see it

You are King of one city, Kreon
That does not give you rights

over the entire Godly earth
The dead do not belong to you

nor the seas nor the soil
You violate the Gods' trust
spilling blood like this
and this blood will double back

when Gaia of the Earth
and Zeus of the Thunderclap
and Hades of the dead
and Dionysus take revenge

Tell me then, Kreon,
come and beg me then
Once women begin wailing
men screaming in the streets
lungs thick with man-made smoke
storm clouds spitting fire

Once all the birds have fled
fish floating on the surface
of the seas, tell me then, Kreon
when all of my predictions
come knocking down the city
that I still speak in bribes

I do not target you for gold
Gold will be worthless sooner than you realise
I speak in science and in knowledge and in reason
So unfold your stubborn arms, old man

snap out of this self-righteous sleep
I am tired of repeating the same warnings
if you keep refusing to hear me
You cannot escape this fate, Kreon
no matter how clever you claim to be

Yes, you are King
This is your decision
I will give you one more chance
to listen.

(argument slows, pace slows)
By the time tonight's moon has danced
a little further through the sky
a life once inside your flesh
will die for what you've done

This is just one of many punishments you'll face,
Kreon
for forcing flowers from light
leaving children rotten on hilltops
for ignoring the warnings of the Gods

*(CHORUS are talking to one another, as if agreeing on something.
They push CHORUS 5 towards KREON, to relay the message/decision
they've made)*

CHORUS 5:
(taps KREON)

King
Please, may I just say

Tiresias, well
he's never been wrong before

KREON:
(strong, then weaker, then resigned)

Yes

CHORUS 5:

So,
perhaps you should take his advice

KREON:

And what advice must that be?

CHORUS 5:

Reverse your rulings
Let Polynices rest in peace
Set Antigone free

KREON:

Give in, you mean?

CHORUS 1:
(stepping to stand beside CHORUS 5)

No, just change

CHORUS 3:
(stepping to stand beside CHORUS 1 and 5)

I agree

108

(One by one the CHORUS step forward to join the others)

Me too
Me too
Me too
Me too

KREON:
(deliberating)

Maybe, I
But then again

CHORUS 4:
(can't hold back anymore)

I can't do this! Politeness isn't working!
King Kreon – everybody is telling you the same
thing.
Listen!

The birds choke
The skies are polluted
The Gods are furious
Do something about it!

(CHORUS 5 sees it isn't really working, continues on a slightly different path of convincing)

CHORUS 5:
(continues)

Kreon. How do you want to be remembered?
The King who sat silent, ignoring the experts

as our Goddess of Earth caved in around him

or the King who saved his entire city from
destruction?

CHORUS 1:

This isn't about him!
This is about us!
We want a different ending!

CHORUS 5:
(gives CHORUS 1 a look to butt out)
Kreon, our time is running out. Please.
Imagine the glory!
Kreon! The King who saved his city!
Who revived the skies; ceased the floods
Your tale will be told for centuries to come
Imagine it! Imagine how your name will be known!
Theatres staging your story a thousand, two thousand
years from now!

An epic of leadership and wisdom and bravery!*
A play about you! A play called *(pause)*
'King Kreon'

KREON:

I'm listening

---

* Emphasise the line which ends 'bravery' so that 'Antigone' is expected as the next
rhyme and the word 'Kreon' is jarring, almost comedic.

CHORUS 5:

Listening is not enough. We need action
This is already happening

KREON:

Ok, I've made the decision
I am King. I *am* the King
Leave it to me

(to the servants)
Men, take your tools to the hill
I will allow the boy to be buried
Remove the rock. Let the girl leave
Give him peace. Give her light
Let the Gods know I'm on their side

CHORUS 7:

Pray the King is quick enough
Pray the Gods are forgiving enough

(CHORUS kneel, faces to the floor)

CHORUS:
(to the rhythm of the Lord's Prayer)
Our Bacchus
Who art in Thebes
Who has a thousand names
Dionysus, Child of Zeus
God of wine and grape
Get us this day away from plague
And re-give us our wines from fields of grapes

As waterways flow by dragon's toothed gums
For yours is the healing
And the dancing
And the music
And the stars

CHORUS 7:

Oh Bacchus
Oh great giver of pleasure

CHORUS:

For yours is the healing
And the dancing
And the music
Please Bacchus
hear our prayer

(Enter MESSENGER)

MESSENGER:

People of Thebes
Forgive me
I have news

CHORUS 4:
(looks up from prayer)

What is it?

(pause)

CHORUS 6:
(to the MESSENGER)
What's the news?

MESSENGER:
He's dead

CHORUS 7:
Who?

(pause)

MESSENGER:
Haemon

CHORUS 1:*
(bereft, but by looking at the others, is comforted)
Haemon? But?

CHORUS 4:
How?

MESSENGER:
A blade
Kreon was there too

CHORUS 6:
What do you mean?

---

* Chorus 1 was relying on the happy ending for this tale; this is the moment she realises it's not coming. A bit frantic, upset.

What did he do?
Did you see what happened?

MESSENGER:

I did. I was with the King
We had almost reversed things
We had reached the hill; found Polynices' corpse
Knelt on the ground, prayed to the Gods
Washed his body. Gathered fresh wood
We burned his corpse
the way it should have been burned
We dug the earth. Recited the rites. Blessed the flesh,
and left

Next, we ran to the cave,
where howling inside echoed like wildfire
The King started screaming,
swore at the skies, shouted:
Is this the game you're playing now? Are you?
Is this a game to you?

He recognised the voice inside, you see,
before we'd even moved the boulder

CHORUS 1:
(sad, to another CHORUS member,
as if giving up the dream)
Haemon

MESSENGER:
Haemon

114

Haemon was slumped on the stone floor beside her,
clinging to her shadow as if Eros might cure all wounds
of this world
Two lovers fallen in each other's arms and he wailed:
Murderer! Murderer! Murderer!
Cursing his father's name
over and over again
as he held her skin against his own

CHORUS 1:
(last dash of hope)

And Antigone?

MESSENGER:

Antigone was already stone cold

We tried to stop the king going in
Told him to give the lovers a little peace
At least let Haemon say goodbye to Antigone
but he wouldn't listen

went rushing in, arms open wide,
wailing 'your father is here now, my boy,
my love',
wailing: 'What have you done?'

With that last question, Haemon looked up
Laid his love softly down, stood up
paced towards his father
until their faces almost touched

breath between them burning
straight into each other's lungs
They stood like that a moment
Haemon staring at his father
Kreon staring at his son

Silence then
Not an echo in the cave
until Haemon pursed his lips;
spat straight into his father's face

I have never seen eyes like that
Lit assassins
Haemon took his sword then
and lunged at his father's heart

Kreon dodged, just missing the metal
and Haemon, despising himself
even more for this miss
braced his own boyish chest

knelt next to his bride
for one final kiss
and fell at her side

Such a bloody embrace
for a young husband and wife

CHORUS 4:
Oh Gods, here comes the King

116

CHORUS 6:

What's he carrying?

CHORUS 1:

Is it Haemon?

CHORUS 5:
(to CHORUS 1)

Don't look

CHORUS 5:
(downtrodden)

Haemon!

CHORUS 6:
(angered)

Tiresias said this would happen

CHORUS 4:

Haemon said so too

CHORUS 1:

Everybody knew!

CHORUS 4:

Everybody except *him*

KREON:

Make way for a useless
fool who never listens
carrying my only living son

My loving son
I loved him
I killed him

I think he's learned his lesson

Too late

You're right
You're right again

(looking at HAEMON and then the skies)
Oh you bastard, bastard death,
I told you I was sorry, didn't I?
Didn't I tell you I would put things right?
I never said I was perfect, it isn't easy being King
But I was trying. Do you hear me Gods?
I was trying!

Why couldn't Hades have waited
just a little bit longer?
Why did you have to take him too? Goddamn you,
God of Thunder, God of Mercy, God of Lies
You already took my wife.
You already took my other son.
Couldn't the God of Anger
have controlled his fury just this once?

Why smash my skull into the soils
when I was already crushed
begging for forgiveness? I beg you again, now,
give me death

(out of breath, slower now)
Let the dogs and the vultures at my bones

CHORUS 7:
You don't make the decisions anymore, Kreon

KREON:
Hide me then. Lock me up
Everything I touch rots
Everyone I love bleeds
I have paid the worst price
for pride and conceit

Fate take me
Let the end come
I am done

(ANTIGONE's body is brought in at the other side*)

(CHORUS come in and move Antigone's body to the centre of the stage instead)

---

* I want this to feel like the end. Haemon and Kreon on one side, Antigone on the other. I'm not sure if Kreon should get up and leave so that it's just the two young people, Haemon and Antigone, lying on the stage at this point for a moment. Otherwise, the three of them.

(The CHORUS then sit around her, as at a funeral)

(The final lines of the play are read by CHORUS 1, standing front centre stage behind ANTIGONE's body)

CHORUS 1:

Once upon a time, two thousand years ago
A young man called Sophocles wrote a play called
Antigone
He ended it with these final lines:

Wisdom is the greatest key to happiness
The laws of Godly Earth must be respected
The big words of arrogant men
will soon come crashing down on them
Wisdom will finally rise

– Sophocles, Antigone, *441 BC*

(In silence, one by one, the CHORUS members stand up, go to a pot at the side, take soil and walk back to ANTIGONE's body, scatter the soil over ANTIGONE and exit the stage. This is done slowly and silently)

(Finally, CHORUS 1 is alone, does the same, then stops next to ANTIGONE, stands for a moment looking around as if to check no-one is watching. She kneels next to ANTIGONE and kisses her like in the fairy tales. She waits, and tries again, as if expecting a miracle. ANTIGONE does not wake up. CHORUS 1 waits a little longer, kisses her one last time, then scatters the soil and leaves)

120

(Only ANTIGONE is now left on stage for the audience to look at, as the song 'Girl on Fire' starts playing softly again in the background)

END

ACKNOWLEDGEMENTS

Thank you, first and foremost, to Sophocles. I hope you are not turning in your grave. Thank you, secondly, to Antigone, whoever you are. Thank you to Alex Clifton and the gorgeous team at Storyhouse for introducing me to the world of Greek tragedy and for being so accommodating to my ideas and queries. Thank you to Natasha Rickman, gem of a director, who made me reconsider this script as we worked towards the first performance. Thanks to Becky Thomas of Lewinsohn Literary, best agency in town, and a huge thanks to Rhiannon and all the fabulous team at Fleet who agreed to publish this in record time. Thanks to my mum and dad for taking me to the theatre and especially for waiting till Jason Donovan was back playing Joseph in *Joseph and the Amazing Technicolour Dreamcoat*. I forgive you for making me wear the red pinafore. Thank you to Michael and Kamila for dealing with me saying I have to work on the final, final edit of *Antigone* for the last year and a half.

Thanks to the people who wrote all of the songs and books and speeches and TV shows and plays and films that maybe morphed into bits of *Antigone* in my head while writing this.

Thanks to Gaia and Eros, now that I know what you mean. In the hope wisdom will rise soon.